Patsy's
Bedtime Stories

ISBN 978-1-62806-432-2 (print | paperback)

Library of Congress Control Number 2024922350

Published by Salt Water Media
29 Broad Street, Suite 104
Berlin, MD 21811
www.saltwatermedia.com

Cover photos by Patsy Myles

Disclaimer: The content written in this book is purely fictional, and resemblance to anyone alive or dead is a coincidence only.

Patsy's Bedtime Stories

Joseph Myles

Author's Note

I hope you will enjoy this collection of stories you are about to read. Bedtime Stories had their beginning while my wife Patsy and I were on our winter vacation traveling around Florida, Georgia, and South Carolina. One night in our campground in Key West after returning from a walk after dinner on Duval Street we got settled in our RV for the night. Right before we fell asleep, I asked Patsy if she was interested in hearing a story, and she said yes. So, on the fly, I made up a tale and told her a story as I made it up. When I finished it she said she liked it, and that she never had any stories read to her as a child.

Needless to say, the following nights Patsy had a new story to hear and fall asleep by. After the first two stories I decided to write the next ones on paper instead of pulling them out of my head and winging it. So that is how this collection has made it into your hands. Have fun with them and Enjoy!

Contents

Sal Olson 11

Day by Day 13

Asset or Liability 16

Serenity Now 21

Brother and Sister 23

Always with You 27

Set Me Free 30

Shucked 33

Glistening 36

Hi Yo Silver 39

Night of Terror 44

Quest of Passion 48

An Empire Rises 54

Choices 57

Old Glory 61

Snowflake 65

The Transition 71

The Twin Brothers 73

What Makes a Grown Man Cry 77

The One 86

The Song 93

Remember the Fallen 94

Have You Ever 96

Memorable Saturday 98

The Art of Dying 104

Sal Olson

My name is Sal Olson and I moved into these new living quarters a few days ago, which marks the start of a life-long career in this newly assigned post. The former resident retired after thirty years of service. I wasn't one hundred percent sure how and if I would be able to follow in the footsteps of the man I was replacing. It takes a special personality to live a daily life without any interaction with another person. Sure, I will be able to see and talk with the delivery man resupplying me with provisions, and removing my accumulated trash, but the time that takes is usually less than an hour, and those people are doing a job and not there for idle chit chat with me. Unless you enjoy being alone in your own thoughts, the time alone can feel as if you were in solitary confinement.

The short three weeks that have gone by were easy for me since I was arranging my stuff after moving in, and getting familiar with my job duties.

Actually the work demand wasn't that difficult, but it was extremely important for the safety of the many that depended on my services. A multitude of people depend on me for their lives to be protected on a daily basis, and yet nobody would know or recognize the name Sal Olson being the guy responsible for providing that necessary service for them. Not getting recognition or credit for my important critical job really didn't bother me. It's just that so many people take for granted the many areas in our lives that individuals are working hard to keep us safe and secure.

Shortly into my third month of duty a very powerful Nor Easter hit our coast in northern Maine. The storm churned up the ocean as no hurricane could. It produced waves up to one hundred feet high. This was a new experience for me, and being so close to the shoreline in my new home, The Crooked Point Lighthouse, would be taking the brunt of those gigantic powerful waves. Every wave that hit my lighthouse reached up to three quarters of the height of the stone and concrete tower structure, and every wave that hit sent vibrations of the powerful pounding impact throughout the lighthouse despite the strength of the structure. Hopefully most of the ships traveling the waters in view of my Lighthouse Light Beacon had already changed their routes to avoid the storm, but nonetheless it was necessary for me to make certain the light still guided. During the storm I was in fear for my own safety at times, and being alone I felt that this was the test to see if I had what it takes to do this job. That first storm pushed me to my limits and convinced me to continue to provide guidance with my beacon for those navigating my ocean.

Day by Day

It has been nearly three days since my last drink. It's not that I am trying to control or limit my drinking habit, it's that I haven't had the money to purchase any alcohol, because I don't have a job. I haven't been able to beg enough money, or steal anything I could trade for some money that would enable me to accumulate the cash needed to buy any type of alcohol. This isn't the first time I've found myself in this position, and unfortunately I doubt it will be my last.

Several times in the past when I ran dry, I had to deal with the same hurdles each time. I'd first seek out every possible source that might give or share with me a swig of vodka, wine, or any other libation I could get my hands on, even cold medicine; whatever would control my visible shaky hands and nervous body gestures. I can usually score a fix at the abandoned garage that three or four of us street people call home.

All of us are in the same situation. We are all going through this dry spell and haven't had enough money to purchase the required alcohol to feed our daily habits. Hank was in possession of the last bottle of vodka he bought after working the traffic light intersection begging for handouts with his "I work for food" sign. But when he left the liquor store, Hank was mugged by a couple of big kids, and they took the bottle of vodka as well as the twelve dollars in change he begged from his day of "work." The rest of us didn't make any money all week because the prized intersection corners belong to those individuals who had established longstanding claimed spots. And a new guy trying to move in on these spots usually wound up getting hurt.

Other methods for begging for money are scarce. We routinely checked the trash bins for discarded unfinished food or a coffee cup with some leftover drips. We always had our eyes focused on the ground in search of any change that might have dropped from someone's pocket, or change that was tossed onto the ground for the simple reason the person didn't want to mess with it in his pocket. We attempted to beg handouts from people coming and going into large stores and small shops. I wasn't very adept at this method and it was a very risky proposition since the cops frowned on panhandling.

Back to my dilemma. I'm actually physically sick from not being able to have a drink for three days. I am experiencing withdrawal symptoms and that bundle of symptoms associated with withdrawal is extremely hard, if not impossible, to deal with by yourself. The alternative which isn't any better, is when there isn't anyone to help you except for the other guys that are in the same shape as you, and also going through the pain of withdrawal.

Thankfully Kurt came through for us. He was able to find a lot of change while crawling under the bank of soda machines in the arcade. After adding that change to the cash he already had, there was just enough for the cheapest bottle of vodka in the store.

When he shared the bottle among the four of us, it was as if we had been stranded in the desert for days without any water. That fifth of vodka was consumed quickly, and it was the medicine we all craved and needed. But all it meant was that we were back in shape with this little fix for only another day.

Tomorrow we will need to start the routine of our endless search of more funds to purchase more alcohol to keep us from getting sick again. A never ending quest to keep us alive. Survival is the best we can hope for. Getting sober and leading a normal life isn't even an option. The hole we have dug for ourselves is too deep and dark to ever crawl out.

Asset or Liability

A nother birthday card has arrived wishing me a happy ninety-seventh birthday. At this age a person gets a lot of cards because people you know whether they be family or friends are so busy with their own lives. They are working and taking care of the many facets of raising a family. So there just isn't much time to visit the oldsters, even on the birthdays. Of course the cards are sent because I have reached another milestone of living one more year—amazing! How many other cards will have to be mailed in the coming years? Don't get me wrong, I do really enjoy receiving all of the cards, I even read them word for word to see who thinks the most of me, despite the fact that the cards are printed with those glowing statements by Hallmark or American Greeting writers. Nevertheless, I still put the cards that elevate how much I mean to the sender in front of the other cards displayed on my table.

Bottom line is that I would always prefer to have a visit instead of a card. And to be able to sit and talk about old times, not their old times, but mine.

I just don't get many visitors these days, mostly because of how daily lifestyles have changed. For instance, in my day most structured sports activities were a school event, and any after school sport such as baseball, football, or basketball, depending on the season, would be played on neighborhood ball fields or basketball courts without hoop nets. Today's world has the kids participating in school sports as we did, but now after school and weekends there is a mass movement of kids of all ages crisscrossing the state in the family cars and carpools. Uniformed kids are delivered to huge complexes of groomed soccer or football fields to play some other county's uniformed opposing team.

There just isn't enough time to do it all. The time it takes to prepare these young athletes to play and compete on the weekends takes time away from the parents. Time they could have used to catch up on the things they wanted to do, or were putting off doing during the week.

Washing and drying the uniforms, feeding them a breakfast to include carbs for stamina, driving them to the destination sometimes hours away, watching the games, grabbing a lunch at times with the team, then driving home wipes out the whole day.

I'm not saying that is a bad thing. It is fantastic for the kids. It builds character as well as promotes team skills. When kids are engaged in sports, the chance of getting into trouble with smoking, drinking and drug use is drastically reduced. Kids playing in team sports will learn how to operate as a single entity, and that will serve each of them well in their future. Team participation promotes developing friendships with others of similar values, and prevents them from mixing with the wrong elements that might lead them into trouble.

When I do get the occasional visit it is usually from my children or grandchildren that have had a break from their busy schedules to take a day trip to see an old man. Sitting around the living room or dining room munching on snacks and taking turns telling stories has to be boring for my grown children and extremely excruciating for the younger kids. I really can't blame them, since the stories are mostly mine. My kids and certainly my grandchildren just can't relate to my stories and experiences in life, and there is no reason why they should. For instance, when I was born, Calvin Coolidge was president of the United States, and I will bet that most people didn't even know he was a president. In fact, if the name isn't Washington or Lincoln, most people are pressed to be able to name the early presidents. Such a shame.

I think my stories are interesting and worth listening to, whether understood or not, and basically that is all I have to share. I can't discuss any subject that has to do with technology, social media, or the modern workplace. I have tried my best to try and keep up with the times. I don't have a smart phone, I still rely on the landline, and my computer is not used for social media nor do I have an e-mail account. So if you don't own the modern devices and learn to use them, you lose touch with the mainstream and are tagged a dinosaur.

This of course places me at a disadvantage when having a conversation with anyone younger than me, which everyone I know is. In many instances I can't even participate. As soon as the conversation includes technology or social media I'm lost and all I can contribute to the subject is my blank stare. Hell, I can just barely deal with the television remote control. And I'm not talking about the menu and settings control—I'm talking about the volume and channel buttons. When my grandchildren start talking about TikTok, all my mind can think about is the tiny mints.

I am in fairly good condition despite being ninety-seven years old. It is true I can't hear very good, and I won't be running a marathon any time soon, but I am still self sufficient. I cook great meals for myself, despite not having the capacity to consume big meals anymore. I maintain and clean my two bedroom fifty-five and older townhouse that I downsized to three years ago.

Although in my mind, I feel as if I was still in my seventies, my two boys thought otherwise and took away my drivers license when I moved into my townhouse. I did hate to give up the right to have a drivers license and the freedom to drive wherever and whenever I wanted. Even though I still felt competent to drive, I gave in without much resistance. I was thinking that I've held my license for eighty-one years without an accident, and I might be forced into giving it up the following year anyway so why not now. A win for the boys.

The next step that apparently was taken concerned my gun cabinet. I noticed my keys to the cabinet were missing. I know they were not misplaced, and I suspected the boys took care of that as well.

I hated losing these rights which meant a lot to me.

Both of those privileges represented a little piece of manhood, at least that is how I interpreted it. But deep down I know my boys were only trying to protect me and keep me safe.

At this time in my life, all of the goals I have set for myself have been realized. I am very satisfied with how I've lived my life, and I don't have any regrets. So I wonder what my future can possibly bring, and how many more years of birthday cards will I be around to receive. Time will tell.

Serenity Now

S tanding alone on the beach before sunrise with my toes caressing the warm powdery sand and facing toward the East looking over the vast expanse of water known as the Atlantic Ocean, I felt in sync with the moment. I closed my eyes, but I was still able to see the water and sky scene I was gazing upon prior to closing them. Standing there I was taking in the soft push of warm air just before the sun rises. The warm gentle wave of warm air displaces the cool refreshing air left over from from the outgoing night.

The experience I was having this morning in the middle of July was only possible for a short time during this time of the summer. I feel the warm calm wall of air that encapsulates my entire body as if the softest blanket was wrapped around me, transporting me to a new unknown place. It is difficult for me to explain how a very minor wisp of warm air could possibly wipe away any and all thoughts that were on my mind before I came down to the beach this morning. The thoughts and noise in my mind from life's daily concerns were gone, at least at this moment.

That transition from a slight coolness on my face, arms and legs to the light cloud of warm comforting air washing over me, puts me in a state of safety and protection likened to being held in someone's arms.

The feeling could not be better. That is until you gradually open your eyes and catch the dark orange sun emerging from the ocean where the water meets the sky.

Already in an extremely mellow state, the visually developing artwork my eyes and mind are absorbing takes my whole being to another level. There is no sense in attempting to capture this show on my camera, although the thought did cross my mind. No camera lens could ever capture on film this sunrise splendor as well as my eyes can absorb and my mind can process.

My moment in time is complete. An outstanding experience, interrupted only by a seagull screeching out a call to another gull.

The sun has now risen and it will soon be getting warmer and then really hot by midday. The beach will be getting crowded with vacationers, but none of them will know of my unique early morning experience.

Brother and Sister

My life on earth has been challenging, but not for that long, since I'm only ten years old. The reason I say challenged is because of the way my life started. My parents were separated before I was even born, so I never had the chance to see or get to know my father, and at the age of five, my own mother abandoned me. I was sent to some facility because I was unable to walk without help. It was discovered I had congenital issues with my spine and other areas of my back, for which I would need surgery. The exact diagnosis is unknown to me because of my age at the time, and if I did know I'm quite sure the explanation wouldn't have been understood. I also was unable to speak since birth, therefore I haven't been able to have a conversation with anyone, and I was having extreme difficulty learning English. With these two major maladies it is easy for me now to know why I was abandoned. The amount of effort it took just to take care of my needs was exhausting, and would only get more demanding as the years went by.

My communication with those around me was limited. I could grunt or make a whining noise trying to respond, but it usually proved to be confusing to those trying to understand me most of the time. Still, my mind was sharp and unaffected by my other problems.

After I had spine surgery my life was in limbo. I was in the facility that provided my surgery, my father is unknown, and my mother is gone. It was a sad time in my life, and I was just getting started. Thankfully an elderly couple took me into their care as foster parents. I'm guessing the couple was in their late thirties or early forties and they could have been my grandparents. They had a daughter that was around thirteen or fourteen years old. I figured out why I wound up with this pair. It was because their daughter was not able to speak either. Sounds as if this was a planned arrangement.

Daily life for me got better in many ways, and more difficult in others. The main advantage I first realized was that I ate regularly, which differed from the days with my mom. She wasn't able to buy us food and there were times I didn't get the opportunity to eat at all. I have no recollection of feeling neglected and I probably thought that was just normal, that is until I got to eat daily.

This new couple even provided me and my stepsister snacks at times, usually healthy snacks, and they did not allow us to have soft drinks or eat candy. Another thing that changed was the house. I now lived in a home that was warm in the winter and cool in the summer. A far cry from those early days with my mom where the priority was to try to find any shelter that put a roof over our heads to protect us from the elements.

In the summer my stepsister and I looked forward to going outside to take in the warm sun rays and play. In the winter we looked forward to the outdoor activities on snow days. This also differed drastically from the early days with my mom.

Six years have gone by since I was able to join this family pod and communication between me and the other family members has improved dramatically. Can't say we share the same language, but it seems we all understand each other eventually.

My stepsister never has totally accepted me for barging in on her life. She was the center of attention for three years before I showed up, and tensions were pretty high at times. Even young blood siblings would have their emotions get out of hand and get into varying levels of confrontation. Stepchildren were no different. In fact our disagreements were probably taken to yet another level. We would get into some real tussles, and she would usually always win.

Thankfully neither one of us would keep a grudge for long, and our disagreement would soon be forgotten.

The one thing we both had in common was that neither one of us is truly sociable. We always had to take time to warm up to someone new. Sis was also much better at that than I was, probably because I was not around many people during my early days. Where Sis would eventually come out of the other room and go greet visitors, I would prefer to keep my distance and go into another room and stay to myself.

My favorite time of the day was when my stepmom would wake up in the morning and make her way down the staircase on her way to the kitchen for a cup of coffee.

As soon as she hit the steps she would begin calling out our names, "Kitty, Sampson, where are you?" And we both would be patiently waiting at the foot of the stairs waiting for our rubs, cat treats and her attention.

Always With You

Heading home after putting in a solid ten hours at work and another two hours traveling to the job site after a very early wake up in the morning, I felt weary. I still had another hour and a half to go before I was to arrive home to my wife and two kids, both girls. Getting up at 4:30 every morning causes the daily lack of sleep to build up as the week goes on. This particular day I already had plans with my wife to take the girls out for dinner to our favorite taco restaurant in order to celebrate Gwyn's birthday. As tired as I felt I was still looking forward to our family dinner, and drinking one of those twenty-four ounce frosted mugs of Modelo Negra draft beers.

I didn't see it coming, I was driving through the controlled traffic signal intersection of Elm and Main streets on a legal green light signal when a Ford pickup truck came speeding through the red light, and plowed into the passenger side of my car at full speed. The force was so great that my car was pushed sideways across the street until it landed against a parked car on the opposite curb destroying that car. My vehicle looked like a pretzel, and I was pinned by the steering wheel and the dash. The air bag deployed and helped to soften the impact to my body, but I don't remember much after the initial impact.

I don't recall anything about how I was removed from the car. But I do remember a little bit about the ride to the hospital in an ambulance, probably because of the screaming siren.

While in surgery at the hospital I died on the table. That's right I'm telling you I died on the table. I have seen the following scenario many times played out on television. You know what I mean, the reported stories from those people who have died and come back to life. They would say "I saw a bright light in the distance and moved toward it" or "my body was there on the operating table and I was hovering four feet above my body observing the scene." Well I felt and saw the same identical things. I had no feeling of any pain, and I was able to hear everything happening. I looked down at my body lying on the operating table and observed everything happening in the operating room.

After the doctor in charge announced my official time of death I had no further use for that room. I have no idea how it happened or how much time had passed after leaving the operating room, but I found myself, or whoever I was now, at my house where my wife and girls were in a hysterical state of anguish, crying and sobbing uncontrollably.

They were asking each other all of the questions impossible to give answers to. Why did this happen to us, and how is this even happening, and is this even possible. All questions that will never have the adequate answers to allow them the calm and comfort they need now. No answer they will hear will give them back their husband and father.

After hours of grieving they were able to start to become relaxed and were tired and drained from dealing with their emotions. It was very late, but none of them wanted to go to bed and lie down to sleep, so my wife decided to fulfill our earlier plans of having a birthday dinner because she said that is what Dad would have wanted us to do. Instead of going to the taco restaurant she heated up some leftovers she pulled out of the refrigerator. My wife put one candle on Gwyn's birthday cake and lit the candle. Gwyn closed her eyes and made her wish. That wish could not and would not be granted. She opened her eyes and started to blow out the candle, but before she could, I put out the candle.

I can't come back to them as wished, but I will always be with them.

Set Me Free

It has been determined through research that my species is one of the smartest creatures in the world's oceans. It is true that my brain is larger than most of my neighbors swimming in the water around me, and I do display many characteristics that indicate superior brain functions. Most of us Dolphins swim freely in large communal groups in every ocean around the world. Our look varies at times depending on which part of the globe we live, but we are basically alike. We are all mammals that nurse our young, and we all need air to survive in spite of the long duration we are able to stay submerged.

Within the large communal group we have smaller family units that are very attentive to each other, and we do like to play when not in the pursuit of food. As with every other living creature on earth, except for humans, most of the available hours in the day for daytime hunters, or night for night time hunters, are consumed with seeking food for our basic existence. This fact doesn't vary for any of God's creatures, except for the human as noted, from the lowly ant to the gigantic sperm whale.

As dolphins we have developed unique skills to fulfill our dietary requirements. Our brains have allowed us to locate an area that has an abundance of small fish, and to work in unison with my fellow dolphins to coral the scattered small fish into a compact dense bunch. This is accomplished by swimming in large circles around the area of the fish then systematically swimming in smaller and smaller circles causing the bait fish to gather together into a smaller tighter and tighter group within the middle of our concentric circles. When the fish are gathered into a dense mass, then all of the dolphins begin to swim through them devouring the fish until only a few stray survive. After that feeding frenzy is complete, we all have our hunger satisfied until we do it again for the next meal the following day.

My life is so much different from some of the dolphins captured over the past years that are placed in aquariums for entertainment and profit, or placed in restrictive small tanks to be used for research. Some of us are put in a small pond that is fenced in under water to prevent us from escaping. This enclosed pond allows paying humans the unique opportunity to swim with us dolphins.

None of these cases allow the captured dolphin to use their learned and inherited skills. Limiting the ability to swim wherever and whenever a dolphin wants, prevents our special skills to be applied, and causes the mammal to become neurotic in a short span of time. This can be observed when a dolphin swims back and forth in the same pattern as if pacing back and forth similar to a lion or bear confined in a zoo. Unless an animal cannot live in the wild due to an injury, it should not be kept confined on land or in the water.

Remember, I said it has been determined we are of superior intellect over others in the oceans, so how come no one realizes that fact. Instead we are confined and we are made to swim in small pools of water, and fed baskets of dead fish to eat.

We are smart enough to know that our freedom has been taken away from us. We know that our life has been limited and we are held captive like prisoners by humans, but we committed no crimes!

Shucked

My given name is XAP22R, but I'm known as Maze. I was bred and developed in a research facility in Kent County, which is on the Eastern Shore of Maryland. My sole purpose for existence is to be the best tasting, best looking, and hardiest corn variety that has ever been developed for human consumption. Each of my kernels have been developed to taste the sweetest and be the most tender to the bite. My color was tweaked to have a pleasing shade of pale yellow that beckons someone to pick me up and enjoy eating right down to the cob.

My family origin goes all the way back to the days when the American Indians grew their corn which was a staple in their diet and very important for their survival. From that point in time the characteristics of corn did not change much until the early fifties when researchers began altering the cell structure in an attempt to develop an ear of corn such as me. They were able to make minor advances over the years until scientists mapped the DNA for corn. It's at that point in time when the number of varieties quadrupled, and the human consumer was able to purchase any type of seed corn to match their taste and market demand.

I am from the altered strain of DNA that first appeared

in New Jersey almost sixty years ago. That original sweet corn was a small kernel yellow corn that had captured more natural sugar in its pulp membrane. People loved this new sweet corn and it became an overnight marketing success.

Since that breakthrough with my forefathers, many small iterations to that strain were introduced over the years. Those changes that were made improved the quality year by year, and spun off a multitude of other varieties. The corn seed market flourished.

My particular variety was created by first sowing in a well prepared plot of earth the previous year's modified corn kernels that had been hand picked to be in pristine condition. These kernels promised to produce even sweeter, more plump, pale yellow kernels on a larger ear of corn. The farmers that were given the task for growing this special chosen corn were also hand picked for their farming expertise. These farmers kept the seed production plots of field separate from the other corn crops on the farm to prevent cross pollination. The farmers were given specific sets of parameters for the amount and type of nutrients to be worked into the soil. The consistent make up of the soil was extremely important so it had to be monitored frequently. The reason the plot of seed corn had to have so much scrutiny was because this was a lab located outside in the elements, and control was important to produce the finished excellent end result, that would be sold in little paper envelopes all over America.

Everyone from the guy with the postage stamp sized

garden plot behind his house to the mega farmer with thousands of acres will be receiving little envelopes or drums of the newest modified kernels. After this year's harvest, numerous ears of this corn will be sent to Walmart, grocery stores, and vegetable stands for sale to the public. After the growing season was finished and the corn was harvested, it would be transferred into the many grain silos in every growing region after the individual kernels were stripped from the cobs and dried.

Even with the proper soil preparation, it wasn't easy for me to get here to tell you this story. After the soil was plowed to loosen up the compacted clumps, I was inserted four inches into the ground and covered with dirt. My closest companions, similar kernels like me, were at least six inches away from me on both sides in the row, and there were rows on the lateral sides a foot apart. I had to patiently wait for it to rain in order to get my growing started, but once the rain began, I was alive and growing.

Once I started to grow there was no stopping. I grew fast but it still took nearly three months for me to mature and to be able to be picked off of my stalks, and then removed from my cob, dried, and packaged, after being graded for quality. My companions and myself will be stored until being sold the following season to be planted for the new summer crop.

So that's my life. Next year my greatness might be replaced by someone even better than me, but is that really possible?

Anyway, see you in Home Depot!

Glistening

When I mention that something is glistening, what picture is painted in your mind? Is it a beautiful, thin, clear crystal wine glass sparkling while outside. Or is it sitting by the swimming pool in the sunlight under the protection of the table's umbrella. Or is it a Ruby Red SUV that has just been washed and polished, sitting in the early morning light with the rays catching every speck of gold dust that is in the special shade of red paint which turns the paint finish into a dimensional piece of art that glistens.

Maybe you conjure up a snowy mountain setting with fields covered in snow that has a thin top layer melted by the winter sun, causing the image to take on a mirror quality reflecting the sky off of its glistening surface. Or could it be the stream running through a snowy mountain scene that is hidden under the thinnest sheet of ice.

Ice that is hidden and covered by a dusting of snow. Then breaking out into the open revealing the clear, rushing water underneath the ice. And then exposing the splashing water droplets that explode with brilliance in the bright sunshine. Which is glistening to you?

As you can see our minds respond to words in many different ways, and the images that are painted in our minds vary drastically. Where one person goes immediately to thoughts of a winter wonderland scene, another might imagine the beach with the suns rays reflecting on the gigantic glistening flat ocean waters. The light hitting the waves at a multitude of angles that are ever changing as they rush to shore, and therefore ever changing in our minds.

Why does this word glistening impart such a variety of images in our minds?

One explanation could simply be each individual's life experiences. Each of us has lived and vacationed in different areas of the country with different types of climate, and several types of weather conditions in each of those areas. Whatever influenced us during those times being in the warm or cold climates, whether disliking that environment, or gravitating towards it, gets imprinted in our mind's memories.

So if you lived or vacationed in let's say Maine, and enjoyed the winter skiing and snow boarding, a glistening winter wonderland is the image your mind painted. Conversely, if you lived or vacationed in Florida and loved being bathed in the warm sun, and going to the beach, the glistening waters of the ocean would appeal to you. Of course the opposite would happen if you were an individual that liked being warm and vacationed in Maine during the winter and was cold and miserable all of the time there, you would probably choose the ocean scene. Whatever the explanation, our minds see and interpret words in many ways.

The accepted meanings of words are clearly listed in our dictionaries and are standardized, but the pictures they paint in our minds glistens in many wonderful images of art.

Hi Yo Silver

I was five years old in the Fifties and growing up then, and being a boy, my fascination was with cowboys and their closest friends and partners—their horses. This closely followed interest was sparked by the new tiny television screen that we eagerly watched whenever we could. There were several cowboy hero shows televised, and thankfully my Dad was very much into anything to do with cowboy themes, which increased my exposure to the television shows. I had several cowboy hero's I followed including the Lone Ranger, Gene Autry, Roy Rogers and of course Cisco and his sidekick Pancho. They all had different roles in how they were portrayed in the shows, but all shared two common themes: Good triumphs over bad, and my cowboys were always good. The second was the love of their horses. This bond made perfect sense because in the old days of the early West pioneer times, the cowboy depended on his horse for survival. The horse was his entire tool box for performing heavy duty work, and of course his horse was his only means of transportation.

Growing up in the television western environment pushed me toward wanting to also be involved with horses. I never had the opportunity to own a horse for a couple of reasons. The first was that my family could not afford one, and even if we could, my parents would have to buy five horses because my four sisters would want one too just because I would be getting one. The second reason was that we always lived in a neighborhood and I'm sure Philadelphia laws wouldn't permit me to have a horse parked in our living room. But I always looked for the opportunity to be near a horse.

One of the high points of my childhood was when a street vendor came down our long street in Philadelphia one Saturday morning, holding the reins of a large pony that was following behind him. He would stop at different intervals talking to the mothers that were out on the street. Apparently he was selling the photos he would take of kids in the saddle upon the pony's back. I don't know how much this cost for the service, but before he made it up to our section on the street I had run in to Mom and told her what was happening outside and begging her to let me ride the horse. After she had the chance to find out was happening along with my persistent begging she succumbed. I was sitting in the saddle on the horse's back, and I felt like I was the king of the cowboys.

When I was in Sixth grade, my parents moved to Miami, and after a short time I was making friends with some of the other boys. One of them already had a paying job and he asked if I wanted to help him after school. When he told me the job entailed rounding up several stallions on a small farm, and bringing them back to the barn for the night, I immediately answered yes. I still had to ask my parents for permission, but I told them it was on the way back from school and Greg had been doing the job himself for weeks and it was safe. My parents decided to give me some experience and agreed to me helping him. This was my first opportunity to fulfill my goal to be a real horseman. The very first day of my volunteered unpaid job I had a huge surprise. The stallions, that looked like short wide ponies, did not want to return to the barn in the afternoon. The resistance they showed was substantial. They bit and kicked, and used their body weight showing determination to avoid returning to the barn. You can picture me a kid of around a hundred pounds trying to make a horse that weighed six times more than me do anything it didn't want to do. And I didn't care for the biting and kicking either. That experience differed greatly from being on that tame pony a couple of years prior having my photo taken. I kept that volunteer job for a week only!

My next equestrian encounter was when I was in junior high school when a couple of buddies and I went to John's girlfriend's house in the country where she owned her own horse. I was talked into riding her horse bareback, because that was how she rode it. Well as soon as I mounted him, and before I got settled on his back, the horse took off. But not in the direction I intended to ride him, which was down the grassy driveway. He immediately turned around and headed towards the back of the house where all of the trees with the low growing branches were. I figured out pretty quickly the horse was determined to throw me off of his back. Even with me ducking down behind his neck, I was still getting battered and scratched from the limbs until he was finally successful. Along with the visible injuries, my pride was shattered because I couldn't do what that little girlfriend of John's did every day.

Lastly, a few years later a large group of the friends I hung with decided to go to a horse riding farm in Waldorf, Maryland. We all had our horses assigned to each of us, and when it came to my turn for a horse, the head honcho said he had to give "Spirit" to me to ride since it was the only horse left because of our large group. He told me it was a good horse but was headstrong and stubborn. I foolishly said that was fine. When we were all mounted on our horses we formed a single file line, one horse behind the other, with me and my horse "Spirit" bringing up the rear. This worked for me because the chance the horse would take off passing the other horses in front of him were slim. But I found out there were other things a horse could do to mess up your day. It started as soon as the line of horses headed out at a leisurely pace down the trail away from the barn. One by one each rider and horse left, except for one.

Yep, me and Spirit. Instead he pretended he was a donkey and didn't move a muscle no matter what I said or did. He didn't pay attention to the reins moving, the heel nudges in his belly, nor the giddy up commands I shouted. Finally Mr. Honcho came over to me took the reins and was able to lead Spirit down the trail about a hundred yards. He gave the reins back to me and said I had to show him who is boss. I already knew who was boss, and it wasn't me.

By now I looked down the trail and lost site of our group that was apparently having a pleasant ride. Five minutes more passed before Spirit decided to move, and when he did move it wasn't down the trail, instead he turned and headed back towards the barn despite my pulling back on the reins. Oh what the hell.

What's with horses? In my first encounter with them, I couldn't lead them back to the barn, and now I can't keep this horse away from the barn. I let Spirit have his way and when I dismounted him at the barn and handed him over, I made the decision right then and there to relinquish the joy of horseback riding to others. I am finished trying to be a horseman.

Night of Terror

We were sitting on a plush sofa with decorator pillows, a fashionable round cocktail table facing in front of us, and to one side of the sofa were two leather occasional chairs. We were facing toward the fancy oak bar with five wood and leather bar stools. On the opposite side of the room were another four chairs, of which one set of two matched, but the other two had contrasting colors from the first set. Behind our sofa facing the front entrance and windows were several small tables and chairs available for meals. Located in the front corner away from the entrance was where the band set up. The location of this new cafe was in the town of Berlin, Maryland just twenty some minutes from Ocean City. We first heard of this cafe coming to the area through our friends and favorite band duo Sonny and Josie, whose performances we have been following for years. Yes, at times we have been accused of being groupies because we happen to show up at our friend's venues for many of the gigs they do at many of our favorite haunts for dinner or happy hour. So I suppose we can be called groupies, and that's alright because they play the greatest hits from our past, and they play them well.

We got this early heads up notification of the coming

cafe because the owner is Sonny and Josie's daughter, and they were here playing for the formal opening tonight.

We weren't very hungry but still wanted to get something to munch on while we drank our beverages and listened to the music. So we ordered the fish dip, which was made from a couple of local freshly caught fish, rubbed with a variety of spices and then smoked.

After the fish was finished smoking, mayonnaise was added along with an abundance of fresh dill. It was served with some club type crackers, and small cut spears of carrot and cucumber. To accompany the dip my wife had a Toscano red blend from Italy, and I had a Stella beer.

We were into the band's second music set, and I was into my third Stella when all of a sudden everyone's cell phone in the establishment went off in unison. We all got an emergency alert signal call informing us we were under a Tornado Warning, and we were advised to take immediate action and take cover in the basement or the lowest floor.

Unfortunately there wasn't a basement in the cafe, and this was the lowest floor. So since we had finished our drinks, I went to the bar and checked out. We waved goodbye to the band, dropped a tip in the jar and headed out the door to go home.

We lived about twenty-three minutes from the Cafe and the height of the Tornado Warning alert for our area was in eight minutes. So that meant leaving now would put us on the road at night during the Tornado activity. When we were leaving the Lounge Josie had an alarmed look on her face not believing we were actually going out into the Tornado danger. I told her we would be okay.

When we got to the car which was thankfully near the front door, it began raining, and within minutes of starting the car and heading home the lightning light show had begun and steadily increased in severity. We continued because at that point we were committed and there was no other choice. In a severe rain storm you can slow down or pull over until it subsides, but that doesn't work for a Tornado. I did drive much faster than usual, and I was even prompted by my wife's urging to drive faster, and she never says to drive faster. I considered pulling over under the only overpass between the Cafe and our house, but as I approached the overpass I noticed a vehicle was already parked under the bridge cover, so we continued on picking up speed as the storm increased. While we were driving my wife was on her cell phone with various family members in the area who were under the same warning and reporting as to the times and location of the Tornado warnings. We were approaching Ocean Pines exit when my sister-in-law told us the tornado was to be in Ocean Pines where she lived at 8:58, it was now 8:57.

Oh shit.

All I was paying attention to was my speed and watching any extra wind action on the trees that might occur, and any additional wind resistance to my vehicle. Luck was with us that night. The only thing we encountered was getting drenched from the rain downpour, and being able to observe a majestic heat lightning light show. The kind of lightning that strikes across the sky rather than the dangerous and destructive type that strikes to points on the ground and causes damage.

All in all we had a great time, checked out a new place to have happy hour, listened to our favorite band, got our excitement levels peaked, and arrived safely at home being greeted by our cats who also were traumatized from the lightning and loud thunder.

Life is good!

Quest of Passion

"Andiamo A mangiare" means in Italian, "Let's go and eat." That was about the extent of my grasp on the Italian language, except for how to say, hello, goodbye, thank you, you are welcome, and a few choice curse words. I was seventeen years old and wasn't doing so great in school and I wanted to quit. I thought I would be able to make it through another year and graduate, but I was kidding myself. Each day in school was worse for me than the previous day. I wanted to quit high school, but I had a gigantic obstacle—my parents. Months ago I had hinted about giving up school and they had a royal fit. To say that they balked at the idea would be a huge under statement.

But I was bold, confident, and determined. I had a dream to be a great Italian chef in my own four star restaurant. My plan was to learn cooking skills understudying other great chefs in Italy. What wasn't in my plan was to stay in school for the last year of high school. I figured I could always return to my studies if I fell flat on my face in my pursuit of being a renown chef.

My decision was made to quit school, but now I needed to convince my parents to allow me to quit, leave the country and move to Italy for an undetermined period.

Money wasn't an issue since I had been able to save enough cash to pay for the one way flight to Rome, and pay a months rent for a room I found online. I would have a few dollars for food until I was able to land an apprentice position in one of Rome's larger restaurants.

My plan was to eat my main meal at the restaurant for free with the other employees. My research indicated that was a usual practice allowing the servers the opportunity to learn the taste of the menu items in order to be able to describe the dish and field any questions the customer might ask. This was especially true for new dishes placed on the menu as specials.

That night at dinner I started the conversation to leave school. This was about the fifth time dinner would be ruined from everyone getting angry about the subject, but I had to bring it up again, since my mind was made up and I would be leaving. Surprisingly the conversation was civil, and when everyone finished stating their reasons for quitting or not quitting, my parents said they wanted me to be happy in whatever I chose to do and gave me their blessing and said they would also help with my expenses. I was floored and elated, and then we finished dinner.

Upon arrival at the airport near Rome, and after I gathered my baggage which was a small cardboard box that was tied and bound with line cord, I got in line to process through Italian Customs.

It was my turn to step up to the window and show my passport and airline ticket. The Customs Agent asked me a few questions in English such as how long I would be visiting in Italy, and the purpose of my visit. He also wanted the address of where I would be residing. I gave him all of the answers, but I guess he didn't like them, because another man appeared from somewhere and escorted me to an office without windows. It was explained to me that my paperwork was not in order because it indicated I was vacationing instead of the necessary proper Visa paperwork needed to work in Italy. I also needed a letter of intent and guarantee to hire from a business in Italy prior to leaving the United States.

A few hours later I was allowed to leave the airport with a representative of the American Consulate and headed to the Consulate's Rome headquarters. Once there they told me I had really screwed up, but they were going to work on correcting the mess. I spent the rest of the afternoon filling out new paperwork, taking new photos, fingerprints, and answering many questions. After it all was completed and reviewed, the official handed me my work visa. Going through all of this trouble turns out to have been a good thing, because there wasn't a restaurant in the country or any other business that could or would hire a person without a work visa. So if I had been able to process through Customs without a hitch, I wouldn't have been able to get the American Consulate involved, and I wouldn't have gotten a fast track process on my work visa. So it all worked out for the best.

Since my first day in Italy was almost over, I went to the house where I was renting my room and spent the evening unpacking my box of belongings and getting settled. Tomorrow I would begin my employment search.

Early the following morning I went down to the little stand on the street and grabbed a coffee and sweet roll and began my search. I was surprised how long the process took, where I expected it taking maybe three or four hours, it took me three days and interviewing with eight different restaurants before I landed a job in the kitchen.

The problem was not my lack of skills, because they had no way of discovering that on the interview, the problem was the lack of communication due to the language barrier. The chef that finally hired me was able to speak a few words in English and I got the job.

My job duties in the kitchen were not what I was expecting. I was started out on the pots, pans, and dishware cleanup, and might have stayed in that position if it wasn't for my nose being in every aspect of the kitchen's operation. I thought I was being inquisitive, but most thought I was just getting in the way. My cleaning duties were not neglected and no one had any issues with my work, so every extra minute I had I was watching somebody prepare, or I would volunteer my assistance to anyone that allowed me to touch the food and knives. After a time the head chef noticed my interest and took me off cleanup and promoted me to salads. This doesn't sound like much of a promotion but it was. Every person in the kitchen went through these exact steps including the head chef, and every other large restaurant followed the same procedure. The length of time spent in each position varied, some never make it out of a position level at all.

My plan is to sail through them all, so once my salad

duties were done I was watching others prepare and again asking others if I could help.

It was a fast climb to the next position for me. I loved being in the kitchen and the head chef was showing me how to do stuff above my position. Line chef would be my next stop, then Sous chef.

In my room I had a small electric hot plate and a small skillet that I used against the rules of the house. Whenever I cooked I had the window opened for the food smells to leave, but that deception was short lived because my land-lady smelled the garlic one day and gave me a stern warning to cease. I told her I wasn't cooking for myself. I explained my restaurant job, and that I was trying my new recipe ideas in my room to keep them a secret from others. She was skeptical but believed me, so I decided to go out on a limb and cook in my room once more. I prepared a Fettuccine with mushrooms and alfresco truffle sauce. The moment it was finished I plated it and brought it downstairs to Rita, my landlady. I knew she ate her main meal at two each afternoon, and it was almost one fifteen now. She was surprised at seeing me in her kitchen, but like I said before, I am bold. I took her by the arm and led her to her seat at the table in front of the plate of pasta I had prepared. I got her a fork and large spoon and said, "Mangia." She took the utensils and began to eat. The look on her face instantly changed to a big grin, she couldn't stop thanking me and saying over and over again how good it was.

I was able to continue using my hot plate to perfect my new creations, and sharing the preparations with Rita.

But that came to an end when Rita told me I couldn't cook in my room anymore because the other tenants wanted to have the same privileges I had.

So saying it with a grin on her face she said from now on I could use her kitchen. This worked even better for the both of us.

In the summer of my third year in the restaurant, I was promoted to Sous Chef. This was recognized as a very fast rise to that position. I felt on top of the world and deep down knew that I deserved it. I had worked very hard to hone my knowledge and skills. I knew every aspect of every position in the kitchen, and could take what I have learned to any restaurant in the world.

Six months after becoming Sous Chef, the Head Chef got into a verbal fight over decisions about the kitchen operations with the owner. The head Chef after Seventeen years took off his apron and walked out. The kitchen was at a standstill watching this unbelievable scene. After it was over, the owner turned to me and made me the Head Chef. It just kept getting more and more unbelievable, because I wasn't even Italian. It is unheard of for a non-Italian, an outsider, to be promoted to Head Chef in a large major restaurant, but it just happened. Probably because of the heated argument, the owner acted impulsively. Sure promoting a non-Italian to Head Chef happens in a smaller establishment if the outsider has extraordinary skills. Anyway I'm now the man, and the menu is mine to use to capture the Four Star James Beard rating.

I'm on it!

An Empire Rises

Our advanced civilization is by far the most powerful there has ever been in history. We are very aggressive and tenacious in realizing our goal of dominating the world. On a daily basis somewhere in the world there are various lineages focused on invading others by hostile means. We bring war to those weaker than us and use our strengths to disable or kill them. Sometimes we attack individuals we have previously disabled without their knowledge, and they in turn meander among their friends, families, and work associates which results in them becoming disabled or even dying without anyone knowing who was the blame.

We will take over the world by any means possible, and we are making great progress globally. Our forces are formidable, and when one of our attack fronts is shut down by the enemy, we can easily transform our tactical attack methods quickly, and will appear to be an entirely different invader to the enemy. Our conquests are usually focused on the weak, aged, and poor, which gives us the highest chance for success to win the battle.

Large pockets of America, Russia, India, and many smaller nations have felt our wrath and we have overtaken their population and have strong footholds in each area. Our presence is not welcomed by those we conquer, but they are helpless against us. The ability to change the direction of the war by changing our appearance gives us a huge advantage over our adversaries that brings them to their knees.

Our base camp is in China and is where we first started to assemble our vast army. China was the ideal location to form this army and begin our first invasion, because of the enormous number of low income residents living in dense proximity without much medical support for most of them.

Our forefathers were created in one of China's biological research laboratories, and then somehow broke out of captivity, and were roaming freely among the population. What followed was relatively easy to accomplish. We just grew and multiplied quickly, moving from one person to another, increasing in numbers using our unique germ warfare methods, and causing casualties exponentially through the neighborhoods, the cities, and the regions. During that time in early 2019 we brought those human targets to submission very quickly. It was easy to expand our terror because travel was at an all time high around the world, so all we had to do was use some of the captured infected carriers that were flying to other countries, to help us spread our cause around the globe and start new wars in new places. Soon there wasn't a place on earth that wasn't terrorized by our devastation. We crippled their economies, their social interactions, their business and leisure travel and their ability to shop.

Despite the chemical warfare they used trying to eliminate us, we would come back stronger by altering our cell structure makeup. We were winning the fights and skirmishes in the early days of the invasion, but after four years of fighting, and having caused millions of deaths, we are on losing ground and are in jeopardy of losing the entire war.

We still survive in small groups around the world because our enemies let their guard down when they think we are gone and it is safe. That's when we take the opportunity and rise up again. Our adversaries don't realize that even if the chemical attacks are successful to wipe us out now, our latent effect in every individual that we disabled by infection will be carrying our civilization in their bodies for their entire lifetimes, and given the chance we will rise again. Because our nation of COVID is a survivor.

Choices

For decades we have been using the calendar to keep our lives in step with time. We use it to enhance or replace our memories by marking the days most important to us such as birthdays, anniversaries, holidays, and medical appointments, to name a few.

Because of calendars we can monitor the seasons of the year and project the changing weather patterns for each distinct season and what to expect with regard to temperatures, wind activity, rain, snow, or hot weather. The calendar from month to month predicts how the natural outdoors scenes will appear to us. Some calendars even portray a photo on the adjoining page for that month of what you should typically be seeing during those days. With that information, we can form a general idea what the weather might be, which helps us to plan our days accordingly.

Each of us knows which months we enjoy the most, for the outdoor activities we are able to engage in. We have learned over the years that in certain months of the calendar the days are longer or shorter, and the temperatures will be very cold or very hot. It's true we might get caught up in the rain, the calendar can't predict that, but we will at least be relatively certain if the rain will be cold or warm depending on the month.

Whether our interests and hobbies are golf, tennis, and skiing, or that we prefer to stay inside and be temperature controlled working a puzzle, board games, or using the cell phone for social media, it is definitely a personal and individual choice. During those months which are cold and snowy an individual that seeks comfort over activity might relish getting cozy with a book, under a soft blanket, with a television in the background. While another individual sees the snow falling and grabs their snow skis and heads for the slopes. Is one choice right or wrong? Both choices are right, everyone reacts to their particular point of view on each day of each month in each season. It is their choice to live it anyway they choose. We shouldn't judge the person that anxiously gets suited up in the snowsuit and boots to venture outside, or the person that would rather stay dressed in their pajamas with the house heat cranked up content to watch television and sip on a cup of tea. Both are entitled to the choices they each made.

Conversely the same differences arise when the hot summer months, the calendar months of July and August. I might wake up early in the morning anxious to get outside and start on my chores, such as grass cutting or working in the garden. Or cranking up the boat for a cruise around the bay or a little fishing. I thoroughly enjoy being outside on a hot day.

The person waking up on the same morning to the same weather conditions won't even crack the door open to feel the temperature outside, whatever the weatherman reported on the previous night's news report is all they need to know about the temperature. Knowing that the day will be blistering hot, and to them unbearable to even go outside, they will stay indoors with the air conditioning set to sixty eight degrees, all doors and windows will remain closed. That is their choice to maintain their comfort level, and that is alright.

I am not trying to distinguish which choices are the best for any particular person, since no choice is incorrect. An individual must decide how to live any single day within a month. You should not be judged for any choice you may make. Granted there are volumes of books written that quote research studies stating that one choice is better for you than the other. Research papers list reasons why a person should go outside and be active instead of being sedentary.

In a large sampling of our population exposed to those research results, you will find that support for the research would be split, where some would side with going outside and staying active is healthier, the other side would certainly not agree. It doesn't matter, we are all masters of our own being and can and should make our own choices.

What is the downside of not agreeing with the research. We might not live as long, maybe and maybe not. How many of us have known or observed someones life practices and noted how that person had made terrible choices on how to live such as abusing alcohol, smoking, over-eating, not exercising and partying into the late night.

And even after all of these perceived unhealthy daily practices, we learn that the individual lived into their nineties. Then we justify the longevity due to their DNA makeup.

So we can only make choices for ourselves. You have heard the phrase "Do as I say, not as I do". This relates to the double standard we live with and practice daily, especially with children. As soon as a child is old enough to be able to walk and go outside by themselves, we make sure they spend as much time playing outside as possible.

It doesn't matter if it is freezing or blazing hot as hell outside, we dress them appropriately and send them out. Rain is the only element that keeps them inside. What is strange is that no matter the temperature, the kids went out with our encouragement, yet we stayed in. If we ever did venture out to play with the kids, it would only be for a short time, and then we returned to our home's comfort.

"Do as I say, not as I do."

So when the children grow to adulthood and have their own children, they will make their choices on rearing their young ones. Will they break the cycle of the past generations, or will they choose to lead by example and have their kids "Do as I do."

Old Glory

An American Sea Captain living during the 1800's was given the American flag by his mother and was so moved by the gift and symbolism he told her he was going to name the flag "Old Glory." William Driver flew that flag on every vessel he Captained until the day he retired. "Old Glory" was retired in Nashville, Tennessee.

That tidbit about the flag is only one of many stories that span many decades in the private and military sectors. Stories of heroism and heartfelt events have affected such a diverse population over the years. The respect we have for the flag is not an easy concept to understand. Could it simply be what the flag colors mean.

Red symbolizes hardiness and valor, white symbolizes purity and innocence, and blue represents vigilance, perseverance and justice. When each of those virtues is elaborated upon you wind up with volumes of explanations and examples of why the flag affects us in the way it does. Combine all of the reasons and we wind up with what we stand for as a nation.

Do you get a little choked up in your throat when you stand facing the flag to recite the Pledge of Allegiance? Do you find yourself standing a little taller at that time also? Do you dwell on the words while reciting the Pledge? I do, and ever since my school days I have felt moved in a curious proud way, even though I had nothing but history studies to cause that feeling. When I served in the Army during the Vietnam years I carried a small American flag with me when going into battle. My intention was not to plant the flag after overtaking a hill from the enemy as demonstrated in Iwo Jima in 1945. I carried that small flag for what it stood for to me. It was a privilege to serve in our military and fight our enemy to promote our ideals of democracy and protect the freedoms for all of my friends, family and fellow Americans that were proceeding with their lives back home. From the day the Declaration of Independence was signed, many thousands of men and women lost their lives while serving with our armed services, in the many wars fought in many regions of the world. They made these sacrifices in order to protect our freedoms, and make it possible for our citizens to live in the greatest country in the world.

Because of these sacrifices we are allowed to engage in any lawful act, at any location, as much, as long, and as often that we want. We have the right to practice any religion in any church without any condemnation for our beliefs. We can endorse any political party that aligns with our values and political bent.

We are the "United States." Those two words are often used as a title name for our country, but take a moment to dwell on what those words mean. The word United let's us all know how we got to this point in history with all of our liberties. Our forefathers were successful in forming our country's formal structure because they were united. In 1776, they were able to meld the ideas and potentials of the country's greatness by voting state by state and becoming united states.

Unfortunately we find our country under pressure here in the 2020s. Our nation isn't as united as we are meant to be. Our right to elect our leaders is still intact, but we as individual voters have been split in our ideas of how we want our leaders to do their jobs.

Not having a unified creed, or a clear desire of how or what we want our elected leaders to endorse in Congress, we can't expect them to be effective in their job duties, and should not to expect any progress in legislation. Our country is split almost in half, as evidenced by recent presidential and congressional elections. We are treading legislative water, and we are going nowhere fast. Why we as a population are so divided on our ideas as to how our country should be run, and who should run it has been discussed by think tanks and analysts for years without coming to conclusive answers. Except for blaming the media for the enhanced slants on the reporting, and the spin on every issue, there have not been any solutions for this malady.

The two political party's actions and personalities are portrayed differently as observed by watching CNN or Fox News. This method of reporting has been practiced for years. But what is different now is when any particular election is over and the winner is not the individual we backed for the office, support for that person is withheld from that time forward instead of lending support to the office that person was elected.

We can all agree that every elected office's main responsibility is to further the American dream and protect our freedoms. This hasn't been the case lately because the elected leaders have spent a majority of their time defending their every move in hearings and press conferences, therefore no progress is made.

Most people acknowledge we are split in our views on our country's direction, but have no fear, we will experience a turnaround that will align us once again. The love of our country, our flag, and our anthem will keep us strong, and I believe there will be an event or string of events that will once again solidify our unitedness.

The flag is our steady reminder of who we are as a nation, especially when the flag is stored or is to be presented. Etiquette dictates how it must be folded in thirteen folds with only the blue stars showing when completed, and each fold is assigned a special meaning. The thirteenth fold reminds us of our country's motto: "In God we trust."

And He will unite us again!

Snowflake

Wish I had a window. Day after day I stare at the four walls in this small eight-by-eight room located three floors below street level.

When I raise my head to take a break from staring at my work spread out upon my desk, all I see on the mostly blank wall is a large calendar pinned directly in front of my desk. This type of calendar was meant to be used as a desk pad for protection of the wood finish. That is why mine is on the wall as the finish on this desk has been gone for a long time. The wall to my left had a twelve inch round black rimmed clock with a white face that I found myself gazing at wishing it was the end of the work day. It reminded me of my early school days when I used to stare at the clock in the classroom waiting for the end of the school day. The wall on my right was where the office entry door and overhead light switch was located. The wall behind me was where I went crazy with my decorating skills. I hung an eight-by-ten inch picture frame with a photo of our President. It wasn't a signed photo, nor did it have any special meaning to me. It was just the official government issue that was distributed to most of the federal offices. Other than my desk chair, there wasn't anywhere else to sit, and why should there be. In the last twelve years, I've had only one other person step into my office, and he was only delivering a memo from my department supervisor. All of the communication I had with my fellow workers was by computer and text messaging. I wasn't asked to attend meetings, and my lunch I brought from home was eaten at my desk in my office.

All of the people I had interactions with in the Agency knew me as "Snowflake" which was my code name. When I started with the Agency, I was told never to use my given name at anytime on anything pertaining to work, but to use my code name instead. I actually thought that was pretty cool back then. It was almost like being a secret agent. Maybe I'll be working with a James Bond type and he'll come to my office to get his assignments. But of course I was being delusional and so far from reality. No visitors ever came to my office, and if I didn't get a reply from my outgoing communications, I would believe I was forgotten and nobody knew I existed.

My work duties did include some highly sensitive information about key economic reports that were released monthly. I did have a top secret clearance because of necessity not to reveal any information to the public prior to the predetermined date and time. These reports were highly guarded to prevent the information from leaking out to the world before that precise time. The importance for preventing an early leak of the economic numbers in those reports could allow some unscrupulous investors to take advantage of the stock market by buying or selling shares of stock in companies that would increase in value up on the news, and reap untold fortunes in profits.

For years, the secrets have been kept without a flaw. No accidental leaks have occurred, and there haven't been any complaints reported of anyone profiting from early information leaks. The system works.

The system works until April's numbers are released next month. I am scheduled for retirement in three months, and I have been working on a scheme for a few years to get back what "They" owe me for being locked down here in my dark little office for all of these years. I suppose "They" is the government, which is an entity without a face or feelings, and can be taken advantage of because the government has enormous wealth and won't miss a little.

My scheme was straightforward. Prior to delivering, I would interpret the economic numbers report, then invest all of my accumulated savings I had held in my stock market brokerage account in those companies that had the most to gain with the direction of the market after the numbers release. No matter if the numbers were higher or lower I was going to make a fortune.

I felt confident I could pull this scheme off without any repercussions because nobody knows my name anymore, I'm Snowflake. No one even knows what I look like, I'm invisible and unknown. I won't be missed by anyone at home or at work.

I have had a brokerage account from the first day I started with the Agency and have been an active trader in stocks over those twelve years. All of my retirement savings are invested in the market, and I have accumulated a sizable portfolio. Therefore a large purchase of a couple of stocks that would increase in value dramatically overnight should not raise any red flags. From my stock research and monitoring certain company stock movements during prior number releases, I know which stocks will rise under those conditions.

After my huge stock play I will put my retirement papers into the system for processing. When I leave work for the last day I will move to Florida and buy a condo on the beach that has all windows and sliding glass doors. I don't have any worries about my crime being discovered from anyone blowing the whistle on me because there isn't anyone. I never married and there isn't a girlfriend anymore. And as I mentioned before, my social life at work did not exist. There wasn't a person that would notice any change of my lifestyle, or even care.

When the numbers were ready to be announced the following day I got busy with my due diligence and chose JP Morgan and Goldman Sachs to purchase. I called my broker, who by the way had no idea what I did for a living, and bought a large position in each of the stocks.

The following day after the numbers were released my two stocks soared through the roof. I was rich. My plan was to let the huge win just sit in the account for months or longer so as not to bring unwanted attention to my actions. Besides I had enough money to live on without touching this new stash.

Three months after my illegal windfall, I retired from the Agency, went to Florida and bought a condo on the beach with all of the windows. I felt fantastic, and even though they didn't know, the government paid me for those lonely bleak days I spent at work in that small office with no window. I deserved making a fortune in the stock market after keeping secrets for years. "They" owed me.

I was enjoying my retirement and the beautiful ocean view, not missing that dank little office I left six months prior, when I got a knock on the door. When I answered, there were two men dressed in suits with two uniformed officers with FBI lettering on their shirts. They asked me if I was Howard Baylor, and I responded yes to their question. Next I was informed that I was under arrest under Title 18 of the US Code, Section 798, which prohibits the knowing and willful transmittal of specified classified information, etc., which covers my using secret information for my illegal personal gain.

My trial was swift and very decisive, I didn't have a leg to stand on since the government had pieced my entire scheme together and easily found me guilty.

I was sentenced to thirty years in a federal prison starting immediately. All of my accounts were taken from me which didn't really bother me as much as what was to happen for the next thirty years. I would be spending those years in a prison cell four feet wide by eight feet long. And the worse thing about the prison cell was, it did not have a window.

The Transition

The memories are still fresh in my mind, I have no idea if they will fade over time, or eventually go away all together. But I still remember now, and until I can no longer remember, I will use the memories to the fullest to further my ability to survive in my new life.

What is freshest in my memory, and is the clearest, is my work which was my whole life. From the very early days after my formal schooling, I had the deep down desire to grow the finest grapes, and then process them into the fullest bodied red wine using the Cabernet Sauvignon grape variety that I could bottle and sell.

I studied viticulture in school and then went to Sienna, Italy to do an internship growing and producing wine under a master winemaker. I learned his magic skills and honed techniques which had been handed down through past generations. When I returned to my home town in Napa, California I was able to use my savings and a sizable mortgage loan to purchase a small thirty acre vineyard. The vineyard was run down, and had not been worked for the past eight years. The only redeeming value the property had was twenty-five year vines and the grape variety was the Cabernet Sauvignon. My dream and plan were coming together.

After I went through settlement on the property, I immediately got to work getting rid of the trash and unwanted furniture and performing a thorough cleaning of the house and the wine storage cave. I got the house and cave in shape. It took more time than expected, but progress could be seen daily.

Now that the house was able to be lived in, and the wine cave was able to hold the stored wine, I headed to the fields to work on the vines. I hired four day workers that had experience with vineyards. I showed the workers how I expected the pruning of the vines to be done, and how to work the soil. They followed what I wanted to the letter. It only took us two weeks to get the vines into shape. It was now Mother Nature's turn to work her magic and make those vines grow and produce some fine grapes. While I waited for that miracle to occur, I had the time to get the wine processing equipment prepared for the eventual crushing, fermentation, and bottling process.

I find it amazing how much of these events I can recollect. I am able to recall how satisfied and happy I was building a winery that produced a wine that was sought after worldwide. I don't understand how remembering my memories will help me to cope with or handle my new reincarnated life. The formal human form I had as a winemaker in Napa was a seamless journey for me at the time. I was in charge of my life. My new body precludes me from exerting my free will, and am now a dependent being in this world. I am now subservient to the human race that I was a fully functional member of. That same human race is now the master of my universe. I depend entirely on the human for my shelter, food, health, and everything I need to survive.

I no longer have the ability to go out to the fields and work the soil, trim the vines, or make the wine. Even though I have the memories that remind me of the times when roles were reversed, reality dictates that whenever the humans decide to feed me, and place the plate in front of me, I eat. When I go to the bathroom, it will only be as fresh and clean as the human will provide for me. If I want a snack outside of normal meal times or need a massage, it is up to the discretion of the human.

Now that my past memories have diminished and will soon disappear completely, my only recourse to survive in my new body and my new thoughts that are replacing my previous mind's thoughts, is to warm up to the human race. Not an easy task since my only means to communicate with the human is to rub up against their leg marking them with my scent, or to announce my contentment by purring, and to alert them to a various array of my needs by different inflections of meow. It will be a learning process for sure.

The Twin Brothers

Growing up in Opa Locka, Florida during the Sixties for a boy wasn't the worse thing that could happen. The weather in this suburb of Miami was perfect for an inquisitive young man of eleven years old. The temperatures were warm half the year and very hot the other half, which allowed me to get outside and play and explore for hours.

The weather was so much more pleasant here than from where we moved in upper New York. The north's weather was bitter and icy in the winter and cold during much of the spring and autumn which limited the number of outside play days.

The more favorable weather in Florida provided a boy the daily opportunity to be on the hunt for the vast array of living creatures that abound in the sub tropical climate. There was always something new to be found, whether it was a never seen before lizard, or turtle. The variety of snakes, both poisonous and non-poisonous, kept my discoveries exciting and my interest keen. When you add all of the different insects and furry animals to the mix, we could not run out of things to discover in our neighborhood.

On my street I had several boys and girls that I

considered friends because they were close to my age and they lived near me. I really didn't have a very best friend among them, they were just playmate friends to me that didn't treat me mean, and did not bully me. We played outside around each other, and I did try my best to join in on some of the outdoor games with them, but my attention span was short and I would only participate for five or ten minutes at a time. Eventually when the kids got together to play ball games and chose sides for the teams, I would always be picked last, and later not picked at all. As time went by I figured out I was not a social individual. I preferred to be alone and keep to myself rather than joining the other kids enjoying their play games. If I felt I needed interaction with someone my own age, who would be better than my own twin brother.

My twin brother was a loner and would also prefer to be off by himself, but would always be there whenever I needed him. He was always there to lend help when my mood or emotions soared or plummeted, or if I was losing control of my composure. His words were comforting when I felt down, or encouraging when I was experiencing a temporary meltdown. My confidence level was much higher knowing my brother would be there to protect me by watching my back and being supportive.

The need for me to engage in active team games with the kids in the neighborhood was dramatically diminished because of my brother's presence. I was fortunate to have someone who knew exactly how I felt at any given moment, and always knew what I am thinking at the same time my thoughts were forming. The reason for this shared parallel oneness must be from being twins.

My brother wasn't always around unless I had a need for his help.

For instance in school I rarely saw him or needed him because I would get immersed in my studies when the teacher was in the front of the class teaching. But on some occasions the teacher would give us free time to study on our own. I then got anxious and would begin to panic. When I reached that point, I really needed my brother with me. and he would show up despite not usually being in school while I was occupied in my structured school classes.

Walking home after school my brother accompanied me back to our house. During that walk he would listen to any problems or difficult situations I had to navigate without his help during the school day. I told him about how I got anxious and fidgety several times during the day for various reasons and in different circumstances. I explained that when the teacher stopped talking in the front of the class and gave us time to study on our own, how visibly nervous I became, and how unbearable it became at times without him there with me. But now all is good. I was relaxed and so happy to be reunited with him on our walk home.

My mother was a saint, everyone said so. She tried her best to give me everything and anything that would make me happy and make my life easier. Her efforts to keep me calm and relaxed was a constant job. Mom tried to

75

provide me as much freedom as possible while still being mindful of my safety. She walked me to and from school every day and attempted to engage me in conversation by commenting on the weather, the pretty flower colors, or perhaps a colorful bird flying by, anything that might prompt a response from me. Nothing ever did.

The only conversations I had on my walks to and from school was with my brother, and he didn't have any conversations with mom either. But between ourselves we did discuss what she was saying to me.

When we arrived at school, Mom sometimes talked with my teacher when she handed me over to her for the day. My teacher would say things like what a pretty day it was, or how good I looked in my new shirt. Of course she wouldn't get any response from me either. But I knew it was a pretty day, and I suppose my new shirt did look good. It was strange she never tried to engage my twin brother in a conversation.

Then there were the days my teacher asked my Mom how she was handling her extremely tough job of being a single mom and raising her only child that suffers with Autism.

What Makes a
Grown Man Cry

When I was a child growing up in the early 1950's it was common practice when raising boys to focus on making them tough in order to prepare them for whatever life has to throw at them. Being a male I was constantly being admonished and reminded not to exhibit any sensitive feelings and emotions because that shows weakness. For instance, when I fell off my bike or got hurt in any other way that was bad enough to produce tears, my father's response would always be to tell me to stop crying and be strong. Another response was that I will be alright, so wipe the tears away and get back on the bike or go back to whatever I was doing when I got hurt. Of course, compassion was shown if my injury was the level necessary for a hospital visit.

During that early time period boys were expected to act more like the grownup adults, while the little girls were still being coddled and pampered. The girls were expected to be little proper ladies and were allowed and encouraged to display their emotions openly.

Most boys were raised much differently during that time period, but it gradually changed over the next thirty or so years, until children that were around my age grew up, married and had children of their own. Those new parents had already decided that their children would be raised differently than they were. Instead of building a macho man out of a little boy, they would nurture and protect the boys and the girls equally.

I can't remember ever seeing my father cry or display any emotion other than laughter and joy, everything else was suppressed somewhere deep in his mind. I knew that he suffered with the burden of his childhood memory when his younger brother died in an accident. And even when he mentioned his death at times when he was drinking heavy, his voice would crack but he never shed a tear in front of me or others. Drinking was his method of dealing with what he wanted to forget, and used to help release the pent up feelings when necessary. That was the role I was supposed to mimic, and in some ways I did. In general the effect this type of upbringing had on a boy's life growing up was a changing scenario.

In grade school we were being molded into little men without feelings. When we graduated to Middle School our tough guy reinforcement and our teenage hormones collided and joined together to form a boy that thought he was tougher than he was. And if that boy got into a fight and would experience a terrible beating and lose, he was programmed not to react with any tears or sign of defeat for any injury or hurt he incurred.

In high school the influence of the peers you have decided to claim as your friends determined which path in life you chose to follow. One path was the academic direction, the other was the social.

Following the social route caused boys to pay less attention to school studies and more attention to the importance to forming friendships and partying. The likely chance of being influenced by those friends led to participating in smoking, alcohol and possibly drugs, which led to a downward trend in their lives.

When the boys choice was to dive into academic studies, the result was that their free time was restricted which helped to prevent him from getting into trouble. Friends were also made, but the friends possessed the same values and they shared the same basic goals.

The opposite decisions of the boys indicates how important it is in taking the correct path in life. Choose social, and you will be interacting with others that do not have a clear direction and will have the tendency to get into trouble and possibly lead to getting hurt or injured. Taking this social direction, if you do get injured you need to act tough by not acknowledging the pain and not openly exposing your feelings.

By graduation from High School the path in life is set and not easily changed. The boy that chose academic studies will probably continue to college or follow an opportunity that will enrich his life monetarily and personally. Whereas the social butterfly will probably land a menial job that will provide enough income to buy a car and pay for apartment rent. Any leftover money will most likely be used for food and alcohol. Going out to dinner will not be an option, but if extra money is available it will be used to go to the local bar.

The environment you choose to live and operate dictates what and how much exposure you will have getting into trouble in the form of fights and confrontations. Placing yourself in harmful environments such as a local bar with a variety of mostly men trying to drink their troubles away, will get you hurt or injured. The chance of someone making a derogatory remark to another intoxicated guy is very likely, and that sets up the chance of a brawl. Even if you are only listening to the guy sitting at the bar next to you sharing his story about how hard his life is because of his multitude of troubles, you are being injured. You are being damaged by his hard luck stories while you are trying to drink away your own. The combination of his problems and your own churns all of your negative thoughts to the surface, and tends to suppress any positive mental energy there might be. I believe this happens as a result of the early childhood style of raising a boy to keep his feelings and emotions hidden, and not acknowledge any visible hurt upon getting injured.

When you reach the age of twenty-five, the way you react and deal with aggression as an adult is much different than when you were younger. Also chances of getting into a senseless fist fight is lessened, so having to suppress feelings of hurt and injury is also diminished. At this key age emotions can be exhibited and won't have to be hidden as often. Injuries that might occur as a result from confrontations or accidents will also become infrequent.

Also at this age the showing of emotion is easier but not completely open due to years of purposely keeping feelings pent up.

The remaining area we will always have to learn to cope and deal with is the announcement of bad or sad news. The news that usually causes the most emotional response is hearing about a relative or friend dying. That is a part of life we will have to deal with until our own life's end. It is very hard to lose someone close to you, and at most times unbearable. Someone who never experienced the loss of someone close cannot understand why grieving reaches such an elevated emotional state. I know that when we are born we are destined to die, and everything in between determines what difference your life made to this world. I believe that is true and what happens in between is why we grieve in different ways and at different levels.

A woman can receive a call informing her of the death of someone close to her and she will burst into an emotional crying mess, with tears and continued sobbing. This response is perfectly acceptable because that is how she was raised to act from the time she was a young girl.

Upon hearing the same news, the man immediately attempts to use every tool in his arsenal to control his emotional state. He sets his facial expression to that of a concerned look, without a hint of sadness or pleasure. He certainly does not cry unless he fails to control his composure. The man's insides might be tightening up and ready to burst from the emotional restraint, but he fights it.

A man has had his behavior programmed from early childhood to bottle up his emotions so others would observe strength rather than perceive weakness.

We as frail humans often fail at the expectations others have placed on us. We cannot always be in complete control of our feelings, our computer-like brain operates too fast processing the signals we receive from our surroundings, and sending lightning fast information to various parts of our body instantly. That is why for seemingly no known reason for men and woman feelings surface, and control is lost. This might happen from the brain interpreting a song heard on the radio, viewing a scene in a movie or on television, or even a comment someone made. The brain reacts to the impulse of information and forwards the information in the form of a feeling, whether it be laughter or tears, it happens so instantaneously that you cannot put up your resistance barrier. This happens most often when the subject is death, whether it be in, movies, or shows, or listening to songs about someone dying, or at the actual ceremonies remembering the death of somebody close to us.

The way I have reacted to death has developed and changed over the years. My first exposure to a person dying was my Grandfather in 1955. At the age of six, I remember being more confused than feeling sad. I didn't understand why he was lying there in the casket not saying anything to anybody. I overheard my aunt say that Grand Pop looked like he was sleeping, I wouldn't know since I never saw him asleep. He was always awake when we visited. What I did know was after they closed the lid and took him away I would never be able to see him again, and he would never be visiting ever again.

My next exposure to a death event was when I was in fourth grade when my friend Greg from school had climbed a tall tree and fell onto a chain link fence and died. In school the teacher addressed the entire class about this tragedy and then tried to comfort us by explaining why this happened and fielding any questions from us. That session might have helped some of the kids understand what happened, but it mostly left us confused. The guys knew Greg better than the girls did, but the teacher spent more time and individual attention in order to comfort the girls.

As the years clicked by I lost many relatives, friends and fellow classmates. Through much of the death announcements, funerals, and cemetery burials I maintained my composure and demeanor as per my childhood training. It was 1977 when my father fell off a scaffold while at work and died. I was in a state of disbelief and felt the deepest sorrow and hurt from this sudden loss. The thought of my Dad being gone was surreal and I had to fight to hold back the overwhelming urge to let it all go and break down. The state of shock and disbelief helped me hold my tears back. Until the time I was completely alone I maintained the control for the benefit of my mother and siblings. It was months later when I finally allowed myself the opportunity to break down and cry, but even then I was alone in my car while driving home.

Many more people I had known and were close to me have died since that time. And at this time of my life, the number of loved ones that have died equals the large number friends and family I still have. As I age I feel myself less able to control the display of emotion. It is much harder to repress my feelings to the extent I was able to at a younger age, and I think this is probably a good transition.

The glimmer of hope for the new generations is that children are now brought up to freely display what they feel and the parental units pamper and provide emotional support when needed. My generation will soon be gone, and with it, the hardened way of dealing with life's tragic events.

An example of the change already replacing the old ways is at the service or funeral of a person who has died. The solemn way previous ceremonies had been celebrated have changed to be referred as Celebrations of Life. That service allows the participants to put aside the sadness of the loss and promotes the happiness of remembering the person when times were good while he or she lived. I have to agree the transition seems to be effective in helping the remaining living to cope with the death and to promote getting on with their lives. Even though the death is celebrated as an uplifting event, exhibiting the emotions with tears will surely happen at sometime in the future days, weeks, and years. It might be sparked by a statement someone makes, or a movie, place or song, that you will immediately associate with the deceased person, and your emotions will break loose.

So what does make a man cry? The answer has to be it depends on what generation that boy grew up in, and how your brain interprets the need.

The One

When I was asked if I could have one wish to make the world a better place to live, it didn't take me long to answer. I wish for world peace and enough food and water for everyone to share.

In a perfect world every person would be living at the same level of income, everyone that could work is employed, and all of the research discoveries that would improve the level of life, be shared by all of the countries in the world. Healthcare would be global and free as a result of not having to build each country's military arsenal. The new defense programs would be to police and protect our food sources, air quality, our oceans health, and fighting global warming. The people of the world could just live happily without concerns, and thrive.

As wonderful as that scenario sounds, it will never come to pass. To understand why, we must look back into the world's past.

Our beliefs are the threads of our global society. The strongest of our beliefs are based on religion. Throughout the history of man we have believed in a supreme entity or entities, no matter what the appearance or name of the entity may be. This belief is shared whether the body of believers is the size of an empire, or the size of a small island village, and the resemblances of the supreme entity or entities are similar throughout the world's populace.

The ancient Egyptians believed in thousands of gods and goddesses. These many gods and goddesses guided the Egyptian people for everything in their lives, such as how they treated each other, how they conducted their daily lives in work and leisure, and how they viewed their afterlife.

The ancient Druids belief was the natural world. They considered trees sacred, and had special respect for nature. The Druids believed in the afterlife, and that when you die the mortal soul left the body, and reappeared into the body of a newborn child. They believed in a supreme god called Be'Al, which meant "Source of all beings", but they also worshiped many lesser gods.

Cultures from the ancient Egyptians to the ancient Greeks had many different belief systems. The Greeks worshiped many gods and goddesses, which influenced every aspect of human life. This belief transcended church and state, and their gods had human appearances. There wasn't single god. Instead many gods and goddesses were revered.

After the Greeks, the next influential leaders of the known world were the Romans. The Romans also believed in a multiple group of gods and goddesses. Within the Roman Empire there were Christian and Judaism religions which believed in only one God. These smaller religious sects that didn't consider themselves to be under Roman domination, presented an irritation to the Roman Emperor, and therefore faced constant persecution.

After many years of turmoil and loss of lives, the Roman Emperor Theodosius issued an edict which made Christianity the official religion of the Roman Empire. By doing that it made all of the smaller start up Christian sects illegal.

Judaism was not affected by the edict, but the Jews were still targeted to be eliminated if possible by the Roman Emperor. The Jews believed in one God, and they followed the teachings of prophets, with Moses being the most important. They believed the Messiah, their Savior, was yet to come to earth.

During the same time period the Christian movement was growing and adding followers. They also believed in only one God. They believed God would send his son down to earth from heaven to teach the population and then give his life for his followers in order to allow them to be admitted into heaven where God resided. It was necessary for him to die because he took all of the sins of the world, including Adam and Eve's Original sin, upon himself in order to save all of us from eternal damnation.

In another part of the world the followers of Islam believed there are no gods or goddesses, only God, and Muhammad is the messenger of God. They also believe in other prophets such as, Adam, Abraham, David, and others.

The main differences in Christianity and Islam is that Christians believe Jesus was the Son of God, and Islam believes Jesus was one of the most important prophets of God, not divine, and not part of the trinity.

In those early times, religions took many separate paths of worship, and many similar factors can be seen in each. Minor changes have been made over the centuries, and the resemblance from one to the other is different, but still very much alike. Smaller sub groups have been intertwined within the larger in many cases, but some have continued on their own paths of worship and have grown, such as Buddhism and Hinduism. There are a multitude of smaller pagan tribal sects that are isolated on islands and in jungles all over the world that still follow the same religious structure the others practice.

Even with the disparities, each of the religions, no matter the size, believe in a supreme being, and the majority refer to that being as God. For thousands of years people have agreed that the creation of humans, animals, insects, trees, and everything that we can observe on earth and the universe, could only be possible with a supreme entity or entities.

The changes over the years on who we believed, and how we decided to practice those beliefs took many turns and directions. What influenced the most change was the act of war. The rulers of many empires used their size and might to conquer others for various reasons, such as land grabs, the riches of others, and prisoners who became slave workers. The Holy Wars continued this plunder in the name of God, and severely affected the world balance at that time.

The Jews have endured persecution for their beliefs throughout their existence. From ancient times they have maintained their beliefs, and those that had opposing beliefs have attempted to eliminate those Jewish believers. Their numbers have diminished but not the strength of their faith.

In our modern world the opposition to another persons faith continues. Christianity and Islam religions preach love and peace, and the majority of followers from each believe and practice this preaching. But in every religion there are radicals that are always trying to promote their twisted altered ideas upon others by extreme methods, such as terrorism. Unfortunately their cause is further promoted by the media which is always seeking sensational news around the world. When politics and religious ideologies causes mix, the differences of each get muddled and warped out of shape, and believing in love and peace becomes secondary to some. As stewards of the earth, do we need to seek peace and love towards all people? The answer is of course yes. Will we ever find and make that peace happen. I doubt it.

At this time peace is out of reach for the world because the inequity of wealth for the worlds population has such a disparity, and as long as the spread of wealth between the poor and the rich is so wide, there will be war and terrorism. It is natural to want the better life that others have, and the only way they think that will happen is to take it by means of force. It would take major reform from governments, and sacrifices by the wealthy to allow the very poorest of the world to rise up to the middle class.

In all fairness this effort has been in progress for many years in America with very little forward motion and success considering the vast amounts of money thrown at various programs. Why hasn't more gain been accomplished. There are several reasons. An example: say the United States identifies a South African nation that has a majority of its population living at the poverty level in need of emergency assistance. In order to help that nation, a congressman has to draft a bill noting the need and urgency of that need, and the amount of funds being asked to send to the nation. The bill goes back and forth between the House and Senate until an agreed upon bill is passed and signed. The money is then appropriated and assigned to an agency for distribution. At times the appropriated funds are not sent directly to the nation, but rather it is used to purchase food and supplies by another agency. The transportation of those supplies are gathered and loaded for shipping by a different agency. The scheduling for the shipment is developed by yet another agency.

After all of the logistics have been satisfied, weeks have gone by. When the supplies finally reach the African nation, the political party in charge of that nation, appropriates the shipment and warehouses a large portion for their own use. The bulk of the supplies will be sold on the Black Market, and eventually be resold to the poor in need. The very same individuals the supplies were meant to be given free in their time of need.

This travesty occurs over and over because the need

around the world is always present. And there are always a few leaders willing to do anything to gain wealth, even threaten the survival of others.

Unless we provide for the poor to be able to help themselves obtain shelter, and to get work in order to lift them out of poverty and into the middle class, there will never be real lasting peace.

If peace cannot be reached, the world's populations can never follow their faith, and can never thank their God for what they have.

The God we each pray to in our many ways appears different to each of us, but I believe there is only one supreme being, and we all are praying to that entity in our own way.

The Song

I wanted to write a love song
But somehow knew it would turn out wrong
Decided to try and see
Thinking how hard could it be
After all it's only a tune
Just a few words that rhyme
I might use words like moon or loon
Everything will be fine
I must remember the rules
You know the ones learned in schools
Sure dove rhymes with love
But so does the word glove
What is it I am trying to say
Could it be what is important today
All I really want to do
Is to compose a verse or two
If I use a few choice words
Will I also need better chords
Did I just write a song
Or only a poem-that is just wrong.

Remember the Fallen

We are a very patriotic country and most of it's citizens have or had family members or friends serve in one of the military services. It is know by all when the National Anthem is played, we stand to face the flag, or music if no flag is present, and remove our hats. What you should do next is confusing to some whether to place your hand over your heart or just stand at attention. I served in the Army and was taught that when in uniform we were to stand at attention and salute the flag. When we were in civilian clothes we were to stand at attention and place our right hand over our heart. Unfortunately this knowledge is not well known, but should be. Over many years I have observed people standing slouched over, others looking all around, some with hands in their pockets, and others still carrying on conversations. None of that is respectful of our flag.

In earlier days we started our school classes daily with the pledge of allegiance and a prayer. We were taught to face the flag or music, place our right hand over our heart, and recite the pledge. Because of that early training everyone knows what to do in that instance. So it is necessary to extend the education for the Star Spangled Banner protocol. It would be great if we all were on the same page with our pledges.

Another area of confusion concerns the greeting given to one another on military based holidays. Although it is straightforward wishing someone "Happy Thanksgiving," "Merry Christmas," or "Happy Easter," but how do you address Veterans Day? A little education on the meaning of the holiday must be known, just as we learned the meanings of other holidays.

Veterans Day is celebrated to honor every military veteran, and the greeting is simply, Happy Veterans Day. Memorial Day is where it gets confusing for some on what greeting to use. Memorial Day is celebrated to honor all of those individuals who served in the military and paid the ultimate service for our country and citizens with their lives.

I have heard so many different greetings for this holiday, with no greeting being standardized to date. The one greeting that is not appropriate is saying "Happy Memorial Day." It just doesn't work for the obvious reason. These soldiers gave their all, their lives. There is nothing happy about that.

After years of awkward greetings for this holiday, I have settled into just saying "Remember the Fallen". Our celebration of Memorial Day is enhanced by our memories, the presence of the many American flags, the playing of *Taps*, and the multitude of memorial services performed on that special day.

In conclusion, remember two important things to do. Place your hand over your heart when our National Anthem is played, and please don't forget to remember the fallen who have given it all for us to have our freedoms.

Have You Ever

It never happens when planned or expected, and it can not be forced or purposefully be felt on demand. Instead at an unknown moment in time, usually when least expected, and while you are doing your very best to maintain a level of somber composure, something out of nowhere grabs you, and overcomes all of your control and composure.

An overwhelming emotion takes over that is usually spurred by extreme sadness or loss of someone close. The feeling that instantly is triggered by a few words, a photo, or even a scene on television or movie. The emotion occurs in the narrow space of time between your thoughts. There isn't any possible means of avoiding or controlling your reaction to this perceived or mental sensation. It is best just to feel it, live it, and then get through it, So I ask, have you ever felt a feeling growing from deep down in your heart, stomach and lungs all at the same time. The feeling is initiated from something someone said, or perhaps from seeing a video scene that touches your feelings in a dramatic instantaneous way.

It has happened to us all, we got caught with our guard down. We made our best effort to suppress our emotions and feelings during the time we were dealing with sadness or loss. When for no explainable reason, other than a few words, or a picture, instantly brings it all back to the present and raises the moment to the surface of our consciousness. Blame it on our wonderful powerful brain, the ultimate computer that has all of our personal life memories programmed, and is always running at full speed. That's the reason we can never control our spontaneous reactions to the stimulus we encounter in our daily life.

Next time when asked if you have ever felt that deep down pain, just say yes, because everyone has. When that uncontrollable moment occurs next time, don't fight it, just go with it. Let your feelings flow.

Memorable Saturday

Our day began early with a planned agenda. It was the third day of our visit with our son and his wife in College Park, Maryland. The reason for this visit was to lend support for our oldest son who was scheduled to have a surgical procedure at the Washington Hospital Center. His surgery was to start at ten o'clock on Friday, so we arrived at the hospital at eight o'clock as directed for his preparations prior to the surgery. As it turned out he was delayed until after two o'clock when they finally rolled him back into the operating room to begin the four hour procedure.

My wife and daughter-in-law were with me in the OR waiting room watching the status board that monitored each phase of the surgery. After the board indicated his surgery was completed, the surgeon came out and told us what was done in surgery. He said everything went well, and he would soon be taken to the recovery room where we could see him.

Almost forty minutes went by and the status board still indicated our son was in recovery but nobody was coming to take us back to him. We all were very hungry and I decided to find something to eat before everything closed for the night. When I got up to leave, a medical attendant entered the waiting room and asked us along with the four other groups waiting to see their people in recovery, to follow him. The attendant informed us all that there would not be any personnel at the waiting room desk to let us know when we would be allowed to see our recovering patients. That information coupled with the rule all visitors must leave the hospital at eight o'clock, which was less than an hour away, and the attendant also saying we might have to wait until the next day to see the patients we were waiting on, was unacceptable to all of us.

That statement he made opened up a dialogue from all five groups attempting to get clarification on how we were to be informed to go back into the recovery room. Finally the medical attendant took the names of each patient and went back into the recovery room to find the status of each and said he would report back to the anxiously waiting groups.

While that was being sorted out, I left to find food for the three of us. The Panera restaurant in the hospital was already closed for the night, so I was left with the gift shop that was preparing to close. I purchased a couple of small bags of trail mix for fourteen dollars and headed back to the waiting room. Upon arrival my family was gone, and I had know idea where. To make matters worse, our cell phones did not have a signal in that area of the hospital. Fortunately one of the couples told me they took our son to the third floor recovery room, and my wife and daughter-in-law went to see him. I was presently on the ground floor waiting room and I headed for the third floor of a very big hospital. After finding a bank of elevators I rode to the third floor, not knowing if I was even in the right area of the hospital. I stopped and asked the only person dressed in a white medical garment where the operating recovery room was, and he said he was he would show me since he just brought two ladies there. He reversed direction from where he had been heading and we took off down the corridor. At the end of that hallway we walked into a recovery room, and he pointed to a doorway. After thanking him, I joined my family who were at the bedside with our son who was still coming out of the anesthesia effects. It was good seeing him awake and in fine spirits, and relieved he was through that part of his ordeal. By then we only had a few minutes left before we had to leave him for the night, so we all said our good nights and headed out of the hospital for home. We all had made it through the long emotionally draining day with good results.

The following day, Saturday, was another early morning start, but this time we would be picking up our son in a few hours and bringing him to his home to recover and heal. We had calculated his release time to be around two or three o'clock in the afternoon, but we all were surprised when he was released before noon. No complaints from any of us for the early release.

When we arrived back at their house, and they were able to get settled, we made certain they were fine, and not in need of our help. We decided to give them their privacy, and got in our vehicle and headed home.

Our ride home was as expected for a summer Saturday

drive to the Ocean City beach with backups in several of the usual places along the route. I was driving my Toyota 4Runner, and my wife was in the passenger seat alternating activities between Sudoku and the book she was reading. When we were approaching Cambridge, Maryland my wife had decided to rest her eyes from reading, and took a nap. Her nap did not last long, because I picked up a white car in my rear view mirror driving very fast and erratic, changing from one lane to another, and approaching fast. I figured the car would be slowing down since there was no opening for the car to have a clear driving lane to pass in, and we were on the Cambridge bridge which was only two lanes wide, and the thirty-five mile per hour speed limit was just up ahead. I was driving my car in the passing lane and the silver car next to me on the right was a car length in front of me in the slow lane. What happened in the next fragment of time was unbelievable. Instead of slowing down, the white car sped up heading toward the smallest of space between me and the silver car. The driver of the white car had no sense of reality, since the needle he was trying to thread was an impossible feat to accomplish. The space between wasn't even big enough to allow a motorcycle to get through, but he tried it anyway.

His right bumper crashed into the silver car's driver side rear sending that car into a spin hitting the Jersey wall. I hit the brakes hard and must have swerved to the left to avoid the collision and the white car went ahead of me out of control and hit the jersey wall and flipped onto its roof.

In my rear mirror I was watching the silver car

spinning behind us, while also watching the white car skidding down the road on its top in front of us, spewing fluids and causing sparks from the road. All the time I was trying to control my brake and gas pedals in order to stay in the middle of the two vehicles and out of harms way.

Soon both vehicles came to a stop and all traffic behind us came to a stop. In front of us two individuals around high school age crawled out of the white car's driver's window, which must have been open, or perhaps broken. They did not appear to have injuries, and seemed very interested in crawling back through the window of the car to retrieve something. The silver car behind us had two individuals, a man and women, that were out of their car standing. I wasn't able to determine if they had any injuries at that time, but other motorists were attending to them. My wife made the 911 call, and within five or ten minutes the scene was filled with Cambridge police, State police, three ambulances, and a tow truck. The bridge was totally shut down on both sides. The State trooper in charge approached my wife and me and informed us he was wearing a body camera, then asked us if we witnessed the accident. We told him what had happened. He took our driver's licenses, and said he would try to get us on our way soon.

After about twenty minutes the trooper returned and told us the driver of the white car said I had clipped him and caused the accident. Our reaction to what he said was obvious. He took a closer look at our car and recorded what he inspected with the body cam he was wearing. Not seeing even a scratch, he stated that was what he suspected. He also said that was the usual response from a driver causing an accident; they would claim that someone else was the cause.

The man and women in the silver car behind us were taken to the hospital, and the tow truck righted the white car in front of us onto its tires. Another trooper from the K9 unit had his dog walk around the outside of the white car, and apparently the dog detected something, which I suspect was contraband. Another pair of troopers went through a knapsack removed by the two individuals from the white car. A third trooper found a large clear bag, with contents I couldn't determine, and placed it into his cruiser. The two individuals were then frisked by the troopers.

After the tow truck left with both of the vehicles, the lead trooper gave us back our licenses, thanked us for our time, and said we could leave. We got in our vehicle and maneuvered around the police cars and personnel and headed home. The investigation was ongoing, so the bridge was still closed to traffic. So for the next hour traveling home the traffic for us was very light.

Our time delay on the bridge was a little over an hour and a half, not bad considering. Our good fortune on this day was that both of us survived an accident that could have been a disaster. We did not sustain any injuries, and there was no damage to our vehicle, only oil and antifreeze fluids from the white car, and a car wash fixed that. All of us involved in this easily avoidable auto accident are blessed for not being killed or seriously injured on this memorable Saturday.

The Art of Dying

When we die, the lasting mark and impact you leave on the world is minuscule due to the vast number of lives who have gone before us. Consider each life is represented by a small drop of paint. And how we lived our life and how we contributed to the betterment of mankind, determines what color combination made up your paint drop. Further imagine everyone's paint drop is placed on a gigantic canvas. Would adding your drop enhance the painting and add to the story of the world? If your answer is yes, then how you lived your life earned you the bright pigments and hues in your individual paint drop that will add to the canvas and translate into a beautiful painting all will be proud of and forever remembered.

Other Books by Joe Myles

Fury: A Soldier's Journey (2019) is an autobiography in which Joe Myles covers the time he served in the US Army from 1967-1969 during the Vietnam War. Read about his combat stories—stories that have never been shared for fifty years.

Tony Capra: Organized Crime Boss (2024) is a fictional account of one man's rise through the mafia ranks. Follow Tony from his early childhood until becoming a man and discover how this innocent child is drawn into trouble by a seemingly lucrative opportunity that changes the direction of his life's path.

Patsy's Bedtime Stories (2024) is a whimsical fictional collection of short stories that were fabricated for pure entertainment and enjoyment.

www.ingramcontent.com/pod-product-compliance
Lightning Source LLC
Chambersburg PA
CBHW031241260626
47169CB00007B/2396